The String Bean

EDMOND SÉCHAN

The String Bean

DOUBLEDAY & COMPANY, INC., GARDEN CITY, NEW YORK

DESIGNED BY *Marilyn Schulman*

Library of Congress 81-43242
ISBN: 0-385-17135-8
Copyright © 1982
All Rights Reserved
Printed in the United States of America
First Edition in the United States of America

The String Bean

The old woman has lived and worked for a long time, in a dark building, bent over a sewing machine as old as she is. There, she makes evening bags, white and golden handbags, with fine embroidery of pearls and silver fringe; glowing handbags, for festive evenings and elegant ladies.

Every morning and evening, the old woman works. But for a short time in the afternoon, when the weather is pleasant, she puts the spools of thread away and closes her sewing machine. An old-fashioned hat on her gray hair, she takes her handbag—an ordinary handbag— and goes out.

She has followed the same path for many years, through the Tuileries Gardens, which aren't very far from where she lives. She likes to walk in them when there are few people there, at the hours when the bustle of the city is faint and far off. As she walks slowly around the impeccable flowerbeds, she dreams of her childhood gardens, filled with the perfume of peonies and lilac, gardens that have disappeared and are forgotten.

On her way home, she always stops in front of a florist's. There are crowds of beautiful flowers that she will never be able to buy. She looks at them for a while and smells their perfume. Then, with her quick little steps, she goes home to take up her work again.

One evening, near a pile of newspapers and some empty bottles, she sees a discarded flowerpot. She picks it up: it holds an azalea. Or it did. The plant is dead. Only pieces of the blackened stem are left in the soil. Still, the soil is good and the pot can be used, so the old lady wraps the pot in a newspaper and carries it upstairs. A flowerpot. Some earth. Good. She holds the pot close to her body, her eyes shining.

In her room, using a fork, the only tool she
has, she unearths the dead azalea. Then, she takes
from a large copper pan one white bean from
among those chosen for her evening meal; the
roundest, the nicest.

With trembling fingers, she digs a little hole
in the soil in the flowerpot, this rare and precious
earth, a gift of chance. In the hole, delicately, she
plants the bean and fills in the soil. She waters
the seed. Then she puts the pot outside on the
windowsill.

Every day, the old woman dutifully waters
the soil. Then one morning, weeks later,
something catches her eye. She can hardly
believe it.

The string bean has begun to grow.

Every day, even every hour, the old woman looks up from her work to look at her plant. Two green leaves appear, then a third.

But soon after this promising beginning, the leaves begin to fade, as if the young string bean has exhausted itself in springing from the soil.

Perhaps the string bean needs support. The old woman finds a knitting needle and plants it in the soil. Then she ties the stem of the plant to the needle with a piece of yarn.

It is not enough. Sometimes in the morning, before ten o'clock, a neighbor vigorously shakes his rug from the window above. An old rug, filled with unhealthy dust. The woman watches helplessly, as the dust dances down on the string bean. It cannot breathe. Later, more enemies appear.

The neighborhood pigeons seem fascinated by the plant. They often peck at the poor green leaves. The woman tries to chase them away, but there are too many of them; and nothing is more obstinate than a pigeon. She cannot spend all her time going from her sewing machine to the window. The lack of light, the rug, the pigeons . . . yet, she must save the string bean.

The old lady decides to move the plant, but there is not enough sun in her room. So she puts her flowerpot out on the landing, first on a chair, later on the ground, trying to find sun for the string bean. And she keeps careful watch.

But the earth turns, and from morning to
evening the old lady must keep moving the pot.

Sometimes she forgets and neglects it.

Sometimes she goes from her room to the
landing and neglects her work.

Then an idea comes to mind. One walks
dogs and children. Why not string beans?

So she takes her little plant to the gardens.
She hides it in a bag so that no one will see
what she is carrying. In the Tuileries there are
sun and water.

Sitting on a bench each day, she watches the
plant as it starts to become green again.

But these walks are brief, because she must work. Back in the dark building, the string bean again looks sickly. Its leaves fall.

She doesn't know how to cure it. She has tried everything. The upstairs neighbor keeps shaking his old rug and the inquisitive pigeons are back. When she looks out her window, she sees high up a superb blue sky.

Outside it is summer, but in some rooms there is never any summer.

Each day, the old lady counts over and over the leaves on her string bean. They do not increase. The plant wastes quietly away.

So she makes a decision.

Very early one morning she arrives in the
Tuileries Gardens: no one is there. She carries
the string bean in her handbag, along with a little
bottle of water. She must act quickly.

The old woman removes the soil from the flowerpot, and uses the empty pot to dig a hole in the garden behind a little boxwood hedge. Then she plants the string bean in a sheltered place in the midst of luxurious flowers. She waters it from her bottle, and keeps the pot, to leave no trace.

Afterward, satisfied and a little tired, she sits for a moment on the bench.

She rests. She is happy. People walk around her, without noticing her or the string bean. Without anyone knowing, she has saved a plant, a life.

That evening, when night falls and the gardens close, the old lady slowly goes back to her empty room, the room where, from now on, she will be alone. She soon misses the familiar presence of the few little green leaves. So each day, discreetly, she goes to see her planting. Everything is going well. With enough sun and water, drawing new strength from the rich earth, the string bean now grows fast.

She looks after it, and sometimes cleans its leaves. Nobody knows that the string bean belongs to her. This bean plant, out of place amid the rare trees and brilliant flowers, is her own secret garden. She has saved it. And seeing it grow is her compensation, her sweet mystery, comfort, joy. Day and night, the old lady thinks about it. There is, somewhere in Paris, something that belongs to her.

And the string bean keeps growing. Quickly, even too quickly, as if making up for the past. Its leaves increase. It blossoms. The blossoms become seeds. Soon the string bean reaches out over the top of the boxwood that has hidden it and kept it from harm.

One day—a beautiful July day—three men come into the gardens: two gardeners and their boss, a very strict inspector. The two men start to work with shears, then with other tools, planting and pruning, clipping and cutting.

When the old lady arrives, at ten o'clock, she is just in time to see them approach her string bean. Its tender green leaves are leaning out farther.

The string bean is out of line. Its presence upsets the harmony of the design. It is an intruder.

The old lady stays away from the gardeners.
Without moving, very worried, she doesn't dare
rush in, to tell these men . . .
She waits, her heart racing.

Suddenly, the inspector points and one of the gardeners pulls out the string bean and throws it on the ground.

After a while the old lady watches the men leave for lunch. When she is alone, she approaches and gently lifts the broken plant. It is dead and the leaves are already fading.

She looks at it for a long time.

But . . .

The old lady picks some of the string beans
and holds them in her hand like a bouquet.
Quickly she returns to her room. She has brought
back some soil from the gardens, puts it in the
pot, and in it plants three new seeds.

These seeds contain everything that remains
of her hopes. It isn't too late, she knows: nothing
is lost. Everything will begin again, as before;
perhaps better than before. That was only a
rehearsal.

Behind her window, the old lady once again is on the lookout, her eyes fixed on the little pot of earth where the three seeds sleep. This time, she will know how to protect them, when to move them, when to bring them home.

In a few moments, she must go back to work.

But first, a healthy, quiet rain comes from the sky. It rains quietly on the pot and on all of them.

The Story Behind The String Bean

Edmond Séchan has directed many award-winning films, including The Golden Fish, *and was the cinematographer of* The Red Balloon. *In 1962, Monsieur Séchan won the Palme d'Or at the Cannes Film Festival for his film* Le Haricot, *a work that has held a special place in his heart. One day, he believed, it would become a book. In the meantime, the still photographs made during the filming were kept in a drawer in his Paris apartment.*

In 1979, he showed the photographs to his friend and associate Mrs. John Fairchild. She had worked with Séchan on a number of films, and now she carried the manuscript and photographs back home to America, determined to find a publisher.

Monsieur Séchan's genius, Jill Fairchild's faith, and the heroine of the film, as well as the story, captivated the editor and the publisher. Our heroine? Marie Marc, who was in fact a medical doctor turned actress for this one film. Customarily, Dr. Marc traveled in a van bringing medical aid to outlying areas. She died in 1980.

Twenty years after the short film's premiere, the story of the string bean—of a lonely old woman, a growing plant, and a growing love—lives again.